Rakhi (rah-khee): north Indian Hindu holiday celebrating the bonds between brothers and sisters; bracelet symbolizing the holiday

Raksha Bandhan (ruhk-shah bun-dhun): full name of the Rakhi holiday

Shravan (shruh-vun): fifth month of the Hindu calendar

Text copyright © 2006 by Uma Krishnaswami
Illustrations copyright © 2006 by Jamel Akib

All rights reserved. No part of the contents of this book may be reproduced
by any means without the written permission of the publisher.
LEE & LOW BOOKS Inc., 95 Madison Avenue, New York, NY 10016
leeandlow.com

Manufactured in China

Book design by Christy Hale
Book production by The Kids at Our House

The text is set in Sabon
The illustrations are rendered in chalk pastel
10 9 8 7 6 5 4 3 2 1
First Edition

Library of Congress Cataloging-in-Publication Data
Krishnaswami, Uma.
Bringing Asha home / by Uma Krishnaswami ; illustrations by Jamel Akib.— 1st ed.
p. cm.
Summary: Eight-year-old Arun waits impatiently while international adoption paperwork is
completed so that he can meet his new baby sister from India.
ISBN-13: 978-1-58430-259-9   ISBN-10: 1-58430-259-3
1. East Indian Americans—Juvenile fiction. [1. East Indian Americans—Fiction.
2. Intercountry adoption—Fiction. 3. Adoption—Fiction. 4. Brothers and sisters—Fiction.
5. Babies—Fiction.] I. Akib, Jamel ill. II. Title.
PZ7.K8975Bri 2006
[Fic]—dc22   2005031069

*For all the families who have chosen
to make the adoption journey, and all the children
who wait for families and homes —U.K.*

For Perran, my Arun —J.A.

ON RAKHI DAY in August, I tell my best friend, Michael, "I wish I had a sister."

"Why do you want a sister?" he asks. "I just got one. She cries all the time. She can't do anything."

I tell Michael about Rakhi. In India, where my dad was born, sisters tie shiny bracelets on the wrists of their brothers. The bracelets are called *rakhi* too, just like the holiday. Brothers and sisters promise to be good to each other, and everyone eats special sweets.

Michael says that sounds like fun. Too bad they don't have Rakhi day where his parents are from.

In October Mom and Dad say we're going to get a new baby girl.
I'm excited. I figure she'll come home from the hospital, like
Michael's baby sister.

Mom says our baby is different. She is coming to us from India.
When the paperwork is done, Dad will fly there and bring her home.

"Can I go too?" I ask.

"Arun, I need you here to help me get ready for the baby," Mom says.

"We don't know exactly when everything will work out," Dad
says. Then he starts talking about "referrals" and "permissions"
and other things that make sense only to grown-ups.

During winter break in December it's cold and snowy. One day,
when I'm folding paper airplanes, Mom shows me a picture that
has come in the mail.

"This is your baby sister," she says. "Her name is Asha."

It's only a picture, but it feels as if she's looking right at me.

"Did you choose her name?" I ask.

"No," says Mom. "She was given her name when she was born.
Asha means 'hope.'"

"I *hope* she's here for my birthday," I say. Mom says she hopes so too.

My eighth birthday comes and goes in March, but Asha is
still in India.

One Sunday morning I go out in the backyard with Dad.
He checks the bolts on the swing set. He oils the links on top.

I try out one of the swings. It goes high without squeaking.

"We could get a special baby swing seat for Asha," I say.
"Like in the playground."

"We certainly could," Dad replies. "What a good idea."

All spring we wait. More pictures of Asha arrive in the mail, and I make more paper airplanes. I pretend that India is in the living room and America is upstairs.

"Look, Mom," I call. "My plane's taking Dad to India." Then I scoot down to the living room and send the plane zooming back toward the stairs.

"Where's it going now?" Mom asks.

"It's bringing Asha home, to America," I tell her.

Mom smiles and sighs. She gets a faraway look in her eyes, and I know she's thinking about Asha too.

The next morning, before breakfast, the telephone rings. Talking on it makes Dad frown.

"It's going to take more time until I can go to India for Asha," he says.

"Why?" I cry. "That's not fair!"

Mom hugs me. "I know," she says, "but we have to go by the rules."

"When you adopt a baby from one country and bring her to another, there are many government forms to fill out and laws to follow," Dad says. "It takes time."

I go to school feeling sad. I hope the people in India are taking good care of my sister. I try to believe that someday soon she will come to us.

When school is over in June, we get Asha's room ready. We paint the walls. We put in a crib and some baby toys.

I make a paper plane mobile and we hang it from the ceiling. Then I make another airplane, so carefully it takes me twice as long as usual. The plane flies all the way from India, in the living room, to America, upstairs. It only touches down once in between.

This is my best plane ever. I put it safely on the shelf in Asha's room. When she gets here, this will be the first present I give her.

Early in July Mom bakes a birthday cake.

"Wow," I say. "Whose birthday is it?"

"Asha's," Mom says. "She is one year old today."

Aunties and uncles and neighbors and friends come to celebrate Asha's birthday with us, even though my sister is on the other side of the world. We show them Asha's pictures. Everyone says how cute she is.

When Asha comes home, I'll help her open her birthday presents.

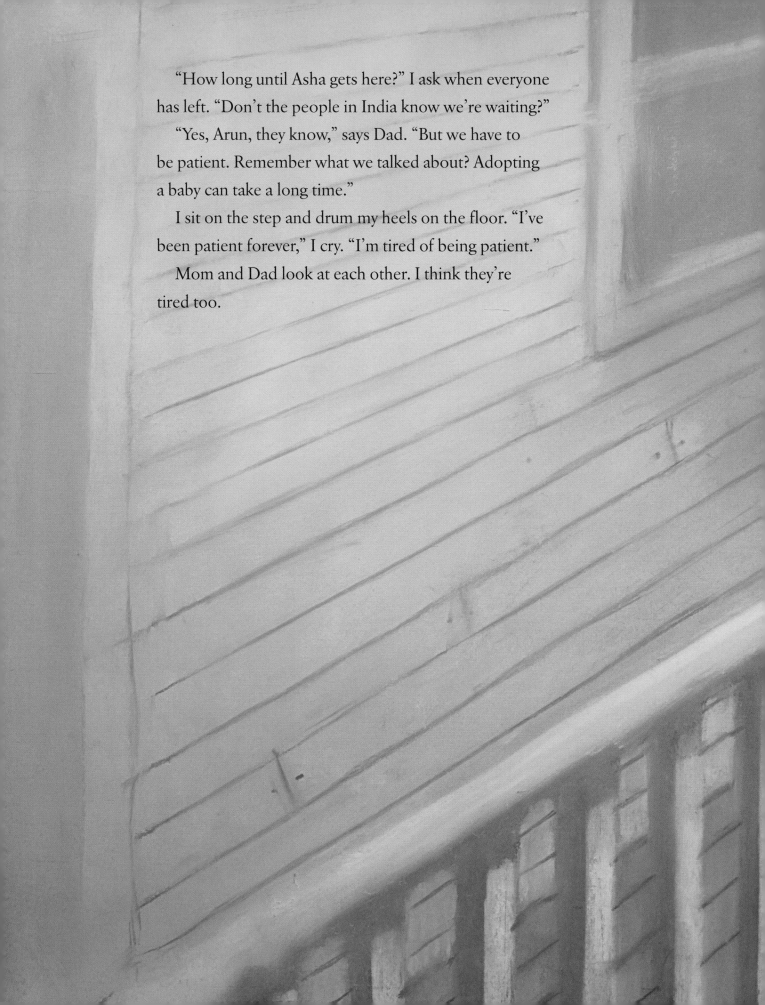

"How long until Asha gets here?" I ask when everyone has left. "Don't the people in India know we're waiting?"

"Yes, Arun, they know," says Dad. "But we have to be patient. Remember what we talked about? Adopting a baby can take a long time."

I sit on the step and drum my heels on the floor. "I've been patient forever," I cry. "I'm tired of being patient."

Mom and Dad look at each other. I think they're tired too.

A few weeks later, on a sticky-warm Saturday, I find an envelope from India in the mailbox. I run into the house and hand it to Dad. He rips it open.

Finally all the papers are ready and signed. The wait is over. Dad can go to India to bring Asha home! I pretend to be an airplane, racing around the room until I'm dizzy.

We help Dad get ready for his long trip. I write colorful letters—forward, backward, upside down—on the folded wings of the paper plane I've been saving for Asha. I tuck it into Dad's suitcase.

While Dad is away Michael comes to visit with his mom and dad and little sister, Denali, who is named for a park in Alaska. Denali is just about the same age as Asha. Maybe they can be best friends, like Michael and me.

Denali wobbles around, smiling. I wonder if Asha can walk too.

All of a sudden Denali topples over. She starts to cry. Michael picks her up and pats her back. "Don't cry," he says. "You're okay."

I hope Asha doesn't cry a lot when she gets here.

Before we know it the day arrives. Mom and I go to the airport. I'm jumpy as a frog, waiting for the passengers to get to the baggage claim area. Finally I see Dad hurrying down a long hallway. He's holding Asha curled up in his arm. I run toward them.

"She's not crying," I say, relieved.

"No," says Dad, grinning. "She cried when the plane took off, but after that she mostly slept."

Asha looks so funny with her little bitty hands rubbing her sleepy eyes. I laugh, and we squeeze into a great big hug.

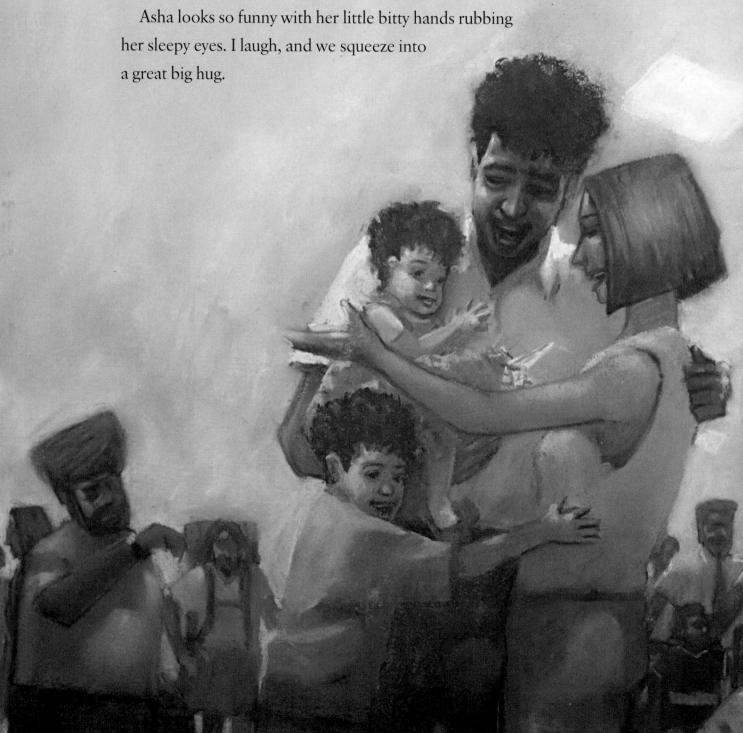

As we leave the airport I see Asha is clutching my paper airplane, a shiny bracelet tied to it.

"It's a few days early," Dad says, "but the people who took care of Asha in India thought she couldn't go home to her brother without a *rakhi*."

Cuddled in Dad's arms, my sister looks so small. Very carefully I touch her cheek. She looks at me and smiles, then holds out the *rakhi*.

"Thank you, Asha," I say.

"She kept it in her hand the whole time," Dad says. "She wouldn't let me put it away."

By the time we get home, Asha is fast asleep. Mom and Dad put her in the crib. I hang my bracelet on my doorknob. I'll wear it soon, on Rakhi day.

I tiptoe into Asha's room and put the crumpled plane back on her shelf. I feel happy and warm inside. My best airplane ever has helped bring my sister home.